T0110954

The Royal Hunt

CHARLOTTE SCHOFF

authorHOUSE®

AuthorHouse™
1663 Liberty Drive
Bloomington, IN 47403
www.authorhouse.com
Phone: 833-262-8899

Published by AuthorHouse 01/26/2021

ISBN: 978-1-6655-1411-8 (sc)
ISBN: 978-1-6655-1410-1 (e)

Library of Congress Control Number: 2021901308

Print information available on the last page.

The Year_Fifteen and Ten
The Territory_Hollowfield
The Castle_Dragonshire
The Village_Edondale

THE PLAYERS
The King_ King Zandor
The Queen- Queen Leah
The Prince_ Prince Vorameer
The King's Cardinal_ Cardinal Rusher
The Cardinal's Alter Boys-_ Toby, Kevin, Gabrial
The Captain of the Guards_ Precious
The number of Guards_ Thirty Nine
Lady in Waiting_ Julie Mandrake
Place of Worship_ House of the Angles on High

THE VILLAGE
Place of worship_ House of the Silver Wings
The Prist_ Father Authos
The Prist's Altar Boys Phillip' Samson, Ian
The Woman In The Village_ Callie
Callie's Daughter_ Glanthria

THE RIVALS

The Territory_The Devil's Mountain

The Castle Dungeons Bay

The Village_ Dragon's Tomb

The King_ King Godric

The Queen_ Queen_ Zarrlonna

The Princess_ Princess Odella

The Captain of the Guard's_ Febus

THE ROYAL HUNTING PARTY

Lord of the woods_ Kendelyn {elvin kind}

Lady of the woods_ Glendoria {elvin kind}

Lady of the lake_ Fandora {mer-folk}

Dwarf male_ Gromic {fighter}

Human Male_Malaki {mage}

Half elf Female_ Frateema {Tracker}

Half elf Female_Veronna {Ranger}

Human Male_ Homri {illusionest}

Wizard Female_ Arigwin {wizard}

WEAPONS

Lord of the woods_ Dagger w/s, shordsward

Lady of the woods_ Dagger w/s shortsward

Dwarf male_ Shortsward {the Purifier}

Human Male_ Battleaxe {Bloodrage}

Half Elf Female_ Two daggers w/s {Deatheaters}

Half elf Female- Bow and arrow {Bow Dragon peircer, arrows Dragons teeth}

Humane male_ Staff of the forest

Wizard Female_staff of the forest

Prologue

The Royal coach is speeding down the dark dirt road. Racing away from the bandits that are in front of them, as well as behind them. A shot rang out from the bandits in front of the coach, and hit the driver in the heart. Just then the horses began to buck, and the coach turned over on it's side.

Queen Leah, and the Prince were thrown into the woods. Thrown against a large tree, and broke their backs and instantly died.

King Zandor was thrown onto the road. The King heard someone say "put the king on my horse and I will take him to the castle.

Was the Royal family a target for assonation, or was the King the target?

Read the royal Hunt to find out.

Chapter 1

The year was the year of our Lord fifteen hundred and ten. King Zandor is on the throne, in the territory of Hollowfield, which overlooks the village of Edondale.

King Zandor, and Queen Leah, were throwing a masquerade ball in the name of Prince Vorameer for his fourteenth birthday.

The Prince is to celebrate his turning from a boy, into a man, and a proper King.

Prince Vorameer is now old enough to put away his childish ways, and learn how to rule his people with a firm hand, but not strict.

The ball was to take place in the grand ballroom of Castle Dragonshire.

Today there are seven Ladies in waiting due to arrive from Mrs. Dansworth's school of graceful charm. The ladies are to be presented to the Queen for a series of tests that the ladies will be graded on. For the lady with the highest grade, she will be presented to the Prince at the Royal ball, as his companion for the evening, and maybe even for life.

Each Lady will be graded on their overall presentation, sophistication, grace, and charm.

First the Ladies were shown into a sitting room for tea and finger sandwiches. Each Lady was graded on her overall etiquette, her vocalization, how she sat in the seat, even how she ate.

After about thirty mins, the Ladies were then taken to the Library and told to find a book of their choice to read. The Ladies were graded on their choice of literature, and again how they sat.

Twenty mins later the door opened and seven Gentlemen walked into the room and approached the Ladies. The Gentlemen then asked the Ladies if they could escort them to lunch.

The Ladies and Gentlemen followed Mrs. Dansworth into a small informal dining hall.

The Ladies were graded on how they walked to the tables, {there were two couples per table} if they put their hand inside the Gentlemen's hand or on their top of his hand, and of course how they sat in their seat. The Ladies were also graded on if they used the right utensils during the meal, and if they used the right goblet for water and wine, even how they interacted with the gentlemen as well as the other couple at their table.

After the luncheon, the ladies and Gentlemen were directed back to the sitting room for some socializing, and coffee.

Mrs. Dansworth left the room to meet the Queen to discuss the Ladies, and to decide which one of the Ladies would be presented to the Prince at the Royal ball.

After thirty mins, Mrs Dansworth walked into the sitting room and said that all the Ladies were exceptional. Their posture was impeccable, and their diction was perfect, but only one Lady would be presented to Prince Vorameer at the ball.

The Lady with the best marks was Lady Juliette Mandrake, since the ball was a masquerade ball, Lady Mandrake was to wear a ball gown, draped in Prince Vorameers favorite color, green, and in clear rhinestones, silver slippers, and a silver mask draped around a bun in her hair. No one was to see her face at all.

Chapter 2

The night of the ball King Zandor, Queen Leah, and Prince Vorameer were standing outside the castle, and a carriage approached them. The carriage was black trimmed in yellow with yellow curtains. It was pulled by only two horses.

Lady Mandrake was instructed to have her mask on before she got out of the carriage.

The driver stopped, then got down and opened the carriage door, and Lady Mandrake stepped out. The driver said "MAY I PRESENT your escort for the evening Prince Vorameer. The Prince walked up to my Lady, took her hand and kissed it.then walked into the ball behind King Zandor and Queen leah.

Everyone who was anybody was already at the ball. Next came the announcement, from the King's. Guard Precious, "MAY I PRESENT KING GODRIC, QUEEN ZORLONNA, AND PRINCESS ODELLA.

The Royal family sat at the table of King Zandor. King Godric had with him his captain of the guards Febus.

To start the ball there was a big banquet. King Zandor asked Cardinal Rusher to give the opening prayer. "We pray oh Lord that you give us the serenity of your love, and the grace to accept these foods that we are about to receive. May this food not only fill our bellies, but give us the nutrition needed to sustain us. We now pray for Prince Vorameer and his parents King Zandor, and Queen leah, for their love and support for this great land. Even for their sacrifices they have made for the land, and it's people. It is in your name we do pray,,,,, amen

Just after the prayer, King Zandor clapped his hands twice, and all the Royal cooks came out of the kitchen one by one with platters full of food.

There were chickens, pigs, turkeys, beef and deer. There was an abundance of ears of corn, bowls of peas, carrots, beans and green beans. There were many kinds of fruits, such as apples, oranges, grapes, strawberries, watermelons, and apricots, and lots of wines red and white.

Of course there were breads of all kinds like cornbreads white bread, wheat breads, and plenty of rolls and muffins.

Just before the music began to start, the court Jester said...

"HEAR YE HEAR YE, THE MASQUERADE BALL WILL NOW COMMENCE. PRINCE VORAMEER AND HIS MYSTERY GUEST AS WELL AS KING ZANDOR AND QUEEN LEAH WILL NOW HAVE THE FIRST DANCE"

Princess Odella told King Godric that this mystery Lady will pose a problem for her, and mess up the plan.

The Princess said "Leave the plans to me, I will take care of the mystery lady".

The Princess walked over to Febus the Guard and said she was going to kill the mystery Lady and he was to bring the Lady to the servants quarters, and that she was going to take the Lady's place at the ball.

The Princess wanted to have Febus go and get the princess a glass of water, but in the water Febus was to put poison in the glass, and tell the prince that my Lady needed to go lay down for a few mins to catch her breath.

Lady Mandrake took the Glass of water from Febus and drank the poison, then fell over into Febuses arms. The Prince asked Febus If my Lady was ok, and Febus said yes she is. My Lady just needs to go lay down and compose herself. Febus then took my Lady to the servant's quarters to the Princess. The Princess then undressed my Lady and put on her dress, did her hair like my Lady, wore her slippers and went back to the ball masquerading as my Lady.

Prince Vorameer asked my Lady if she was feeling better. He had no idea that it was the princess.

The Prince and the now mystery Lady danced all night long together.

King Zamdor soon announced that this was to be the last dance of the night, but told the people NOT to unmask themselves.

Chapter 3

One of the Guards called for the King's carriage. The Royal Family had to go to a special mass that night after the ball, a special Mass to commemorate the passing of Prince Vorameers childhood, and the new life of the man.

The mass was to be held at 11:45 pm, and concluded at 2:15am.

The road that was to be traveled by King Zander's carriage was very long and very dark, and was surrounded by trees and thick woods.

All of a sudden, the carriage started to rock and jerk. The King heard a number of voices in front of the carriage, as well as behind it.

There was a sound like an arrow being fired in front of them, then the Queen saw the driver fall onto the ground. Then the Queen heard a horseman jump from his horse onto the carriage and release the team. Then the carriage turned on its side. The Queen and the Prince were thrown into the woods and landed against a tree. They both broke their backs and died instantly., but King Zandor was still alive. The King was thrown onto the road.

King Zandor could feel blood running down his face, And his leg was caught under a tree limb. His arm was twisted behind him.

The King heard someone say' Take the King and put him on my horse, and I will take him back to his Castle to the doctor.

King godric walked up to King Zandor and said "King Zandor, You almost ruined my plans by dying my friend, but one way or another I will get what is coming to me!.

King Zandor asked King Godric if he knew what happened to the Queen and the Prince, Are they alive?

King Godric said no, they were thrown against a tree and instantly were killed.

My plan was to kill you and take over this territory, after all we are best friends. I needed you to sign over the Kingship to me first, that is why you almost ruined my plans, but that now can be rectified. Then King Zandor passed out.

Once King Godric is back to the castle, King Zandor was then taken to his room and the doctor was called.

King Zandor was found to have slipped into a coma. Princess Odella never left his side, so when King Zandor woke up she would be the first person that he saw.

King Zandor was in a coma for a total of thirty-eight days.

When he woke up, he asked about his beloved Queen and his son. He did not remember asking King Godric at all.

Princess Odella said regrettably they both had passed sway in the accident.

Princess Odella told the King that both the Queen and the Prince flew out of the carriage when it turned over, and they both were thrown against a tree.

Princess Odella said that she was in love with the Prince, so his death was a shock. Both the Queen and the Prince were found the day after the accident, and they were brought back to the castle to be buried.

Chapter 4

The bodies were taken to the royal cathedral just outside the castle walls to be prepared for their royal entombment.

The bodies were striped down, only the royal priests were allowed to touch them. There were priests that were specially trained in the royal customs on how to wash down Royal body's. ONLY The bodies were then put in a bath of rose water and lavender petals. Every inch of the body is soaked down and washed with silken cloth.

No part of the body is to be touching the table NOT EVEN THE HANDS.

A royal autopsy is then performed. Each tool used on the body could only be used once, then after it was used it must be sterilized and thrown into an incinerator. Each tool is kept in a special vault before use for ONLY Royalty.

After the autopsy is performed the body is then rubbed down in aloe and camomile oils that have been blessed by the pope himself.

Now the bodies were dressed in their Royal robes and placed in a clear casket, wax is then used to seal the casket and the Royal seal is placed into the wax.

The bodies are now prepared to be blessed by the cardinal.

This process takes a total of four days to complete.

The caskets were now placed within the center of the village for all to see and pray over.

Two days later the caskets were taken to the Royal House of worship, the House of the angles on high for the Royal Funeral.

It was a small funeral, only King Zandor, King Godric, Queen Zarlonna, and Princess Odella were in attendance.

Cardinal Rusher was standing in the center of both caskets. The alter boys from both churches were on each side of the caskets holding the lighted candles.

Cardinal Rusher then delivered the Lord's prayer.

OUR FATHER WHO ART IN HEAVEN HALLOWED BE THY NAME,

THY KINGDOM COME,

THY WILL BE DONE,

ON EARTH AS IT IS IN HEAVEN.

GIVE US THIS DAY OUR DAILY BREAD,

AND FORGIVE US OUR TRESPASSES,

AS WE FORGIVE THOSE WHO TRESPASS AGAINST US.

AND LEAD US NOT INTO TEMPTATION,

BUT DELIVER US FROM EVIL.

AMEN.

King Zandor, King Godric, Queen Zorlonna and

Princess Odella surrounded both caskets during the Lord;s Prayer.

Then the EUCHARIST was then to observed.

A holy room located just off the sanctuary was where the caskets were then placed.

The Royal altar boys from both churches then carried the caskets to the Royal room.

Now another prayer was said by Cardinal Rusher over the caskets. {again the Lord;s Prayer}

Then everyone left the room except King Zandor and Cardinal Rusher. A benediction prayer was then said.

OUR FATHER, RECEIVE THESE TWO SOULS INTO YOUR KINGDOM. LET THEIR SOULS FOREVER BE IN THY HANDS. WE NOW PRAY, IN THY FATHER'S NAME....AMEN

As King Zandor and Cardinal Rusher leave the sacred room, the door closes behind them and wax is used to seal the room.

The caskets stay in the room for a period of one year.

During that year King Zandor was not allowed to see or touch another woman.

A Black shroud was then placed over the Queen's Royal portrait in the castle, as well as the royal portrait of the prince. The bedrooms of the Queen and the Prince were then locked up and sealed with wax and Royal seal.

Chapter 5

It is now a full year later. The time for mourning is now over.

King Zandor and Cardinal Rusher are now in front of the sacred room in the sanctuary in the House of the Angles on high. The Royal seal is removed, and the room is then opened. A prayer is then delivered by Cardinal Rusher.

"OUR LORD IN HEAVEN, WATCH OVER THE QUEEN AND HER SON PRINCE VORAMEER AS THEY ARE ETERNALLY LAID TO REST. MAY THEY BOTH REST IN PEACE FOR THEIR ETERNAL LIFE IN YOUR HOUSE. IN THY NAME WE DO PRAY... AMEN

Then the Royal alter boy's as well as the alter boys from the village again carry the caskets to a black carriage awaiting to take them to the Royal cemetery.

At the cemetery, King Zandor says his last goodbyes to both the Queen and the Prince.

Now that a year has passed it is time for the King to find a new Queen.

Princess Odella had planned a party for King Zandor for two reasons, one because it was Halloween, and two because King Godric's plan could start to grow.

All the men at the party were dressed up as Frankenstein, and all the women were dressed up as the bride of Frankenstein. At the party King Godric seemed to be pushing King Zandor and the Princess together.

King Godric's plan was to have King Zandor and the princess fall in love and to someday marry, to kill the King, and Princess Odella to take over, with King Godric soon to be on the King's throne. Then King Godric's guards will be stronger, and Hollowfield would be one with THE DEVILS MOUNTAIN AND DUNGEONE'S BAY.

All night long Princess Odella tended to King Zandor's every need. The Princess never let the King's wine goblet run dry.

The King and the Princess danced with each other every dance.

King Zandor got somewhat Tipsy at the party because he was missing his wife and his son who was in line for the throne, so the Princess took the King back to his bedroom, and had his servant put him to bed. The next morning before breakfast King Zandor prayed

OH HEAVENLY FATHER, HELP ME TO TAKE ON THE TASK BEFORE ME. IT IS TIME THAT I LET GO OF MY PAST LIFE, AND MAKE A LIFE THAT IS NEW.

IN THY NAME...AMEN.

Then the King had his breakfast and went to the

Royal thrones and removed the black shrouds off the Queen and Prince Vorameer's thrones.

Then took down the shrouds off of the portraits Queen and the Prince.

Then went to the Royal bedrooms and took off the seal and unlocked the doors.

The black shrouds were then buried. As time had passed Princess Odella had even learned to cook for the King.

Months and months had gone by, and King Zandor grew closer and closer to the Princess. You could not pry them apart.

King Godric was happy his plan was taking effect. One night Princess Odella told King Godric that King Zandor and herself were getting along so well, That she felt that King Zandor would soon ask her to marry him.

It is hard that Princess said to keep playing along when you hate someone so much as she hates King Zandor

King Godric told the Princess to stay strong and remember that you are doing this for your true King.... ME!

It will not be long before you and the King wed, and the good King Zandor will be dead.

King Zandor then approached the Princess and asked her to dinner. The King said he had something of grave importance to ask her. King Zandor had planned a very special dinner for the Princess. It was all of her favorite foods like veal, pasta, with chestnut and peas, salad, and white wine, and pineapple shortcake for dessert.

Princess Odella was wearing a long baby blue silk gown, with long white gloves, and a dark blue rose in her hair.

The King and Princess had their salad and drank their wine, but after the salad course, king Zandor put his hands on the Princess, got down on one knee and said, "PRINCESS ODELLA, I NEVER THOUGHT I WOULD EVER FIND ANOTHER LADY IN THIS WORLD THAT WOULD EVER LOVE ME THE WAY THAT YOU DO, MUCH LESS A LADY THAT I COULD GIVE MY LOVE AND MY HEART TO.

AT FIRST I THOUGHT THAT YOU WERE JUST CONSOLING ME BECAUSE OF THE DEATH OF MY WIFE AND SON, BUT NOT REALLY MEANING IT, I THOUGHT YOU WERE TRYING TO HELP YOUR FATHER TAKE OVER HOLLOWFIELD BUT I SOON REALIZED HOW VERY WRONG I WAS. YOU SHOWED ME A KIND OF LOVE THAT I NEVER THOUGHT I WOULD SEE AGAIN. ANYONE WHO CAN SHOW THAT KIND OF LOVE CAN NOT BE FAKING, SO PRINCESS ODELLA WILL YOU MARRY ME?"

The Princess said YES I will marry you my King!

That night the Princess ran to King Godric's room to tell him that his plan was working.

The day of the wedding, King Zandor had on his Royal Robes, and Princess Odella was wearing a yellow dress with a VERY long train that was carried by two ladies in waiting.

The flower girl was throwing out rose petals for the Princess to walk on.

There were Seven maidens of honor.

The Princess had peach carnations for her bridal bouquet and white lilies on the end of the pues.

Cardinal Rusher at the end of the service said

"MAY I NOW PRESENT KING ZANDOR AND QUEEN ODELLA!"

Chapter 6

King Zandor was playing right into King Godric's hands.

The other part of the devious plan of killing The King can now happen.

Queen Odella told King Zandor that yes she did comfort him at the time of their death but it was really just a ploy, you were right. I really do not care for you and I surely do not love you.

I cried over the Prince because I needed it to look real.

It is a law that no Royality could not get a divorce, so instead King Zandor and Queen Odella Slept in different beds witch was ok because Queen Odella Refused to have sex with the King.

At this point King zandor said to Queen Odella "I MAY NOT BE ABLE TO DIVORCE YOU, BUT I CAN MAKE SURE YOU DO NOT HAVE AN HEIR TO SIT ON THE THRONE'. That was one wish that Queen Odella wanted was a child to sit on the throne.

That night King Zandor snuck out of the Castle

and went to the village. There was a young woman that had gone to pay her last respects to the Queen and the Prince, and he needed to find her. The King thought she was very beautiful and very sweet

King Zandor found the Lady and went up to her to introduce himself. He said "hello there", my name is Zandor, she said I know. You are the King I have seen you. My name is Callie. What may I do for you my King? King Zandor said he saw her at the wake for his wife and son, and he wanted to come and thank you for all she said.

Callie said I have a humble home, but would you like to come in?. The King said thank you yes I would. Twice a week the King would go to the village and see Callie. Soon they became lovers.

Callie became pregnant with The King's baby.

Finally, the day came for Callie to deliver, but sadly King Zandor could not be there because the delivery was during the day, and the King had to stay at the Castle.

There was a problem. Queen Odella had known about the affair for many months now, but did not say anything because she wanted proof first, well now she has it. Callie had a baby girl. The baby's name was Galanthria.

Chapter 7

THIS CHILD COULD SOON TAKE OVER THE THRONE!

That is what Queen Odella told Febus, her captain of the Guards.

I just cannot have a "commoner" Take over MY throne.

No one will ever take the throne away from me!.

The Queen told Febus that she had a plan. She said that she had a special job for Febus, but he would have to hire some good men. No I have a better Idea, said Queen Odella I will hire the men so I know that the job will be done right.

I will send for the best villains of our homeland of DEVILS MOUNTAIN.

The Queen told Febus that once they all arrived, then she would tell them of the plan all at once.

The Queen told Febus that Tomorrow night is Callie's daughter's birthday and she will now be 16.. Tomorrow night I want you to sneak into the village to Callie's home and kidnap the daughter when the clock strikes midnight and the moon is at its highest point. I do not care what you have to do, just do not kill her. Bring her here to me.

King Zandor had no idea that the Queen knew anything about Callie, much less about Galanthria.

That night Febus and the bandits snuck into the village when the moon was high and at its highest point. Callie and Galanthria were both asleep. Febus and the bandits snuck into the house and kidnapped Galanthria and then took her to the Queen.

Queen Odella said 'my my Galanthria is it?, You know you are a very beautiful young lady, but that fact will not help you where you are going. It is a shame that no one will ever see that beautiful face again.

The Queen told Galanthria that her father the King would never find her precious body.. The King can search and search, but he will never find you.

Though you are a Princess yes you will never take the throne. The only thing you will be Princess of is the swamp and swamp monsters.

Now take her away. Get her out of my sight.

The Queen told Febus to take the girl out into the forest DEEP into the forest to the old witch's cabin. She will know what to do with the young Princess.

Chapter 8

⎯⎯⎯⎯⎯⎯⎯⎯◆⎯◆⎯◆⎯⎯⎯⎯⎯⎯⎯⎯

It has been 3 days since Galanthria had been kidnapped Cardinal Rusher approached King Zandor and told the King that he had to discuss a very private, and very important matter.

Father Authos had confessed to the Cardinal that one of the Queen's guards had told him in confession that on the eve of three nights ago someone had been kidnapped. The Father said that this person was to be taken to the witches' cottage deep in the woods. and never to be seen again.

The Queen's guard said that something dastardly was to happen to the kidnapped person as per the Queen..cardinal Rusher told King Zandor that Father Authos had broken confession, but Father Authos did not want the confession hanging over his head.. Father Authos said that Cardinal Rusher would know what to do with the information.

King Zandor called forth his captain of the guards Percious to hire ten of the greatest fighters to be in a royal hunting party, to find and bring back Glanthria.

King Zandor now had to admit that Galanthria was his daughter. That he had an affair with a woman from the village named Callie.

THE FIGHTERS.

1. LORD OF THE WOODS_Kendlyn (elvin kind}
2. LADY OF THE WOODS_GLENDORIA {Elvin kind}
3. LADY OF THE LAKE_FANDORRA{Mer-folk}
4. Dwarf male_Gromic{FIGHTER}
5. HUMAN MALE_MALAKI{MAGE}
6. HALF ELF FEMALE-VERONNA{RANGER}
7. HALF ELF FEMALE_FRATEEMA{TRACKER}
8. DAWARVIN MALE_GRIM{FIGHTER
9. HUMAN MALE_HOMRI{ILLUSIONIST}
10. WIZARD FEMALE_ARIGWIN{WIZZARD}

The day came for the hunting party to begin their quest. They headed into the forest. The first thing Frateema found were tracks of the bandits as well as Galanthria. You could tell that she was being dragged through the forest. At least the hunting party knew that they were on the right track. The forest was filled with all kinds of Bandits, and monsters, so the hunting party knew that they needed to stay alert. When the night came and time to sleep, one person in the party had to stay awake to stand guard. Bright and early the next morning the party came across a band of merchants. Merchants can be passive or aggressive depending on who they come across. Homri asked the leader of the merchants if they had seen a band of Bandits with a young girl go by.

Yes we have seen them, they even killed three of my men.

Homri gave the leader 5 gold pieces for the information. He thanked Homri, and told him to go south into the forest, go towards the village of pandora. There you can replenish your suppplies. There is a witch who lives deep in the forest, that is where the bandits said they were going to take the girl.

Chapter 9

The hunting party moved on towards the town. There, they rested just outside of the town.

The sun was down and the moon was high. Arigwin decided to make dinner for everyone. She made tea, rabbit stew, baked beans, biscuits w/butter and jelly, and blueberries for dessert. The next morning, Gromic and Grim went to the village to buy more supplies, and to nose around, while the rest of the party stayed in camp.

Grim went to the Inn and asked the Innkeeper if there had been any strangers in the village. The innkeeper had said she had not seen any strangers in town, but she heard the storekeeper say that strangers came in and said they needed to buy rations for two weeks. They also said they needed to buy winter clothes and bedding because the forest was getting cold.

Gronic went to the general store to buy supplies, and ask if the strangers were buying a lot of stuff. The store keeper said "there was a man here buying a lot of rations and warm clothing. he said he asked if he was going on a trip because he was buying so much stuff, and the man said he was taking a group of boys into the woods to learn how to hunt, but he wanted the rations just in case to fall back on.

Gromic and Grim went back to the camp and reported what they had learned to the rest of the party. The party decided to leave that day so they would not be that far behind the bandits.

The party didn't see anything for days, but they had heard a girl scream. The party knew that the bandits were close. Frateema the tracker said that the bandits were close enough to smell.

Just around the corner the party found a lake. Homri looked into the lake and saw the outline of a lady, then he heard her sweet voice starting to sing. It was Fandora, the lady of the lake, and she had two dragons wrapped around her.

All there has to be is some kind of water, and Fandora and her two dragons will appear.

A few mins later the bushes started to rustle, limbs started to fall down, and trees were being smashed. There was a loud growl that came from a LARGE cave near the lake.

It was a goblin Rat it had changed forms from a rat into a ratman.

His weapon of choice was a two handed sword. Homri used his staff against the ratman and shined the brightest of lights into the rat man's eyes, and Gromic took his sword {the purifier} and cut off one of the ratman's arms. The light had then gone dim, but just enough for the ratman to swing his sword, hitting Frateema in her side.

Fandora commanded her dragons to breathe an ice storm on the ratman, then Maliki ran up swinging his sword at the ratman and shattered him into a million pieces.

Chapter 10

That night The Hunting party restored, and Fratemma was on Guard duty.

Frateema woke up the rest of the party because she heard something making a hissing noise, then they saw a Giant Spider spinning a web all around them. The Giant Spider could disguise it's voice, so it sounded like King Zandor. The Giant Spider threw its voice and said" The princess is just beyond that tree" You need to go and get her and bring her back to me" Kendyln told the party" NO DO NOT LISTEN! IT IS NOT THE KING, IT IS THE SPIDER TRYING TO TRICK YOU!

IT IS TRYING TO MAKE YOU LOOK CLOSER SO IT CAN KILL YOU!"

Arogwin had an acid arrow, so she snuck up on the Spider and shot the arrow right into its main eye and it fell down dead.

After the party killed the Giant Spider, they all were really hungry, so Kendlyn decided to go hunting and see what he could find

Kendyln ended up hunting down a rabbit, and Verona skinned it, and cooked it over an open fire.

The party also had peas, and berries that they had found in the forest. They even had coffee that they had in their rations.

The next day the hunting party started out again, and walked right into a bog.

They saw smoke up over the bushes, then heard stomping and splashing noises,

Something was coming through the bushes.

Something very large, and very fierce.

It was a typhoon Dragon. The Dragon swung it's leg, and huge claws towards Aragwin.

Aragwin threw a flesh to stone spell, but it only caught its tail.

Fandora threw an ice storm from her staff of water, and it froze the dragon.

Kendlyn then ran up and stabbed the dragon in the heart and instantly killed it.

Chapter 11

Frateema saw an oval looking object out of the corner of her eye so she got up and walked over to it to see what it was,

It was gold in color, and kind of grainy like an egg. Frateema then picked it up, and it started rolling around in her hands.

She took it to the rest of the hunting party and said "look what I found"

Fandora said "that is a gold dragon egg. Gold dragons are good luck for their owner, and since you found the egg Frateema. Then you are the dragon's owner. Fandora said that gold dragons have magical powers. Just then the egg started to hatch.

The first person that the dragon saw was Frateema.

She named the baby dragon Drako.

Draco could talk, and had promised to help the hunting party. but only if Frateema said they needed his help. She was the dragon's master.

The only thing that Drako said he would not do was kill one of his own kind, whether he was good or evil.

If anyone or anything was attacking Frateema then the dragon would defend her to the end,

Later on that day, the hunting party ran into a cave. This cave was full of gems and weapons, even magical weapons, and a staff.

Frateema asked Drako if he knew, who, or what lived there, and he said yes a relative of mine a topaz dragon.

The topaz dragon became fast friends with Frateema. He told her that he would protect her as well, and he would help his kin the gold dragon in anyway that he could.

The topaz dragon's name was Bastille.

Bastille gave each person in the hunting party eight gold pieces, three silver shillings, and four rubies. There was a village just on the west side of the cave, so Maliki went to the village to buy rations, while the rest of the hunting party went to the Inn to clean up and rest.

After the party cleaned up and rested, they went down stairs to have a good meal.

The party had chicken, baked potatoes, carrots and blackberry pie for dessert. They even had elvin wine to drink.

After the meal, they went upstairs for the night. The hunting party thought they would get a head start in the morning, so they could gain some time on the bandits

They walked about half a day into a very dark and dank part of the forest. There were a lot of dead trees and bushes, there were huge rocks everywhere, and Giant Vultures flying all about.

There was even an ogre running around.

Homri happened to look down at his feet, and

coming out of the marsh was a gold magical ring with a black stone in the middle.

It was a ring of feather falling.

One of the Vultures flew down and took Gromic in its tallens and flew him up into a nest with 5 babies up in the tree.

Arigwin cast a spell of invisibility on Gromic, as Homri cast a spell of feather falling on Gromic. Gromic jumped from the tree away from the hungry baby birds.

There was another problem. The Ogre was stomping around yelling GET OUT OF MY BOG! Homri also had a ring of spell turning, so that any spell that the Ogre tried to cast would be rebounded back on him. The Problem was the Ogre had a spell of protection upon itself.

Arogwin said stand back, let me try something.

From the Staff of the Forest. She said one word WRAP. The spell was put on the tree closest to the Ogre.

A beam of light shined out of the staff and onto a very thick vine, and it wrapped all around the Ogre over and over. The vine wrapped around the Ogre so many times that the Ogre tripped and fell to the ground.

Then, Kendelyn cast a spell of sleep on the Ogre, then Verrona just walked up and slit its throat and stabbed it in the heart to make sure it was dead.

As for the Vultures, they saw the dead Ogre, so they flew down and started eating it. The momma took some of the food back to the babies.

Chapter 12

────────◆◦◆◦◆────────

A few yards away was a small hut. The back door of the hut began to open, and out walked the Queen's Guards, and behind them was the old witch hag.

The hunting party ran behind some trees to hide. The old hag had black stringy hair, wrinkled fingers, super thin legs {like a chicken lol.},

Her arms had wrinkled skin hanging everywhere, green eyes and a LONG fat nose. Her shoes were curled like the witches have in cartoons. She had a shril in her voice, and when she laughed she crackled.

She had on a green short dress {pea green}, and two big dogs that sounded super mean.

Gromic got close enough to hear the witch say,'you do not have to worry, I will take real good care of the young Princess my Lord's. Tell your Queen that she is well taken care of, No one will ever find her!

Even if someone were to cast a find spell, or any kind of spell for that matter, No one will ever see her precious face again!

Chapter 13

The hunting party knew that when a fight ensued it would be a battle of all battles, wits upon wits, so they all had to step back and re-group.

The hunting party had the advantage because the Queen's Guards did not know they were there.

The Queen's Guards knew that King Zandor would have hired people to hunt down the bandits and take Galanthria back to him, but The Guards did not know that King Zandor hired the best trackers and fighters in the land.

The hunting party had all their animals in readiness.

Aragwin had made a large body of water, so Fandora, and her two dragons were also there.

One of the spells that all dragons possess is the spell to shrink and grow large.

The hunting party was as ready as they will ever be. Homri threw the first spell. He cast light into the bandit's eyes hoping to take away their sight.

It worked on all the bandit's but one. He looked away as soon as the spell was cast. Aragwin cast misdirection on the bandit, and he ran straight into a THICK tree and it killed him instantly.

Since the rest of the bandits were blind, the hunting party could sneak up and stab them in the heart one by one.

Arogwin used her spell of healing on Homri.

One of the bandits was hanging onto life, so Glendora's brown bear Balto leapt at the bandit and slashed his throat with his razor claws, but the bandit held his double edged sword over his head and slashed at Balto cutting his throat wide open.

Frateema asked her gold dragon to blow fire on all of the bandits' swords to melt the swords down for the silver.

Now that all of the bandits were dead, the real battle is set to begin!.

Chapter 19

The old witch yelled at the hunting party, "WHOEVER IS OUT THERE I WILL TELL YOU NOW IF MY DOGS DO NOT GET YOU MY OTHER PET WILL, AND THAT IS MY SERIOUSLY LARGE BLACK DRAGON." To bad the girl will be his next meal.

The hunting party's magic had to be top notch to battle the witch and her so called pets.

There were five people in the hunting party that could use magic

1. Kendlyn
2. Glendora
3. Fandora
4. Homri
%. Arogwin

Homri was putting more spells into his staff, so he was not able to fight once the fighting started.

The staff was given to Kendlyn.

Glendora also had a staff that she found hidden in the rocks.

All weapons were ready to go.

Everyone needed to rest, so the party rested for the night. Glendora used her spell of invisibility around the party, and the camp.

The hunting party decided to have rations for dinner so the smoke can not be seen or smelt.

Even though it was very cold out, there was not to be a fire for the old witch to see.

Early the next morning the hunting party was getting ready to fight when the witch came out the back door followed by Galanthria holding a basket of laundry.

The witch was yelling "HANG UP THE LAUNDRY GIRLY, HURRY UP OR I WILL SICK THE DAMN DOGS ON YOU.

When Galanthria was done the witch yelled "NOW" GET IN THE HOUSE GIRL."

The hunting party yelled at the witch "IN THE NAME OF KING ZANDOR, YOU NOW MUST REALISE THE GIRL TO US AND WE WILL LET YOU LIVE, OR YOU MUST PREPARE TO DIE."

The witch said "YOU CAN NOT HAVE THE PRETTY LITTLE PRINCESS, IN FACT YOU WILL ALL DIE BEFORE YOU CAN TELL ANYONE SHE IS HERE."

The witch threw a phantasmal killer at the hunting party, but Glendora's staff detected the spell on the witches hands, and Glendora cast spell turn immediately and the witch could not cast the spell at all.

Kendelyn threw a freezing spell on the witches

hand's so she could not use them, but the witches eyes could cast spells, so she could cast a killer spell, back. Sadly Gromic got in the way and was killed instantly.

The witch cast a pass without a trace upon herself, and got behind the party. The problem was then the witch cast drain energy spell on kendelyn so he could not cast any magic for a while, or so the witch thought.

Kendelyn surprised the witch and cast a spell to copy himself and the person the witch encountered. The witch tried to throw another phantasmal killer at Kendelyn but it did not take.

The witch cast a spell upon herself of return, and was at the cottage. She ran inside and downstairs to the black dragon and released him

The first thing the dragon did was breath fire on the hunting party, but glendora put up a firewall around the hunting party so the fire could not touch them.

Glendora reversed the spell, and burnt the witch's hands.

There was a spot next to the black dragon where kendelyn cast a water spell and Fandora appeared with her two dragons.

The two dragons cast Ice Storm on the Black dragon, so the typhoon dragon along with Fandora from her staff.

Malaki appeared next to the black dragon and slammed his swords into the black dragon's heart, and the black dragon broke up into thousands of pieces.

The witch ran back upstairs and locked the door behind her.

The gold dragon cast a shrink spell upon itself, and walked into the lock of the door and unlocked it.

Kendelyn went inside and found the witch hiding in one of the rooms, but she did not see him.

Kendelyn cast a globe of invisibility upon himself as soon as he got into the hut, but the witch knew as soon as the magic was used.

Frateema found the witch's magic potions, and stole a poison potion, gave it to Glandora because she was making tea for the ol hag

Glanthria put the poison into the witches afternoon tea hoping she would not smell it.

The witch came out of the room, because she thought she heard a strange noise. So the tea had gotten cold. The witch yelled at Glanthria" GIRL, WARM MY TEA IT IS COLD NOW."

So Glanthria warmed up the tea.

The witch drank the tea and yelled. "GIRL YOU USED MY OWN MAGIC POTIONS ON ME AND POISONED MY TEA!"

The witch fell to the floor screaming in pain, then just died.

Glanthria ran up to Kendelyn and threw her arms around him and said "THANK YOU THANK YOU. AM I GOING TO SEE MY FATHER SOON? "Kendelyn said, "Yes my dear you will soon".

Chapter 15

There was a town a couple of miles away, so that is where the party decided to go for much rest. When the party got to town they had gone to the hotel there, got a room and went to get the rest they needed.

After they rested, they went down to the hotel restaurant to have a good meal. They ate rack of lamb, spiced potatoes, rye bread w/butter, and mincemeat pie with honey mead ale to drink. After the meal they all went upstairs for a well deserved rest.

Glanthria shared a room with Frateema.

The next day, Grim and Frateema went to the general store to buy more supplies for the trip home., and they put the supplies in their room.

The rest of the party went to scout out the town.

There was a festival in the center of town and they were holding an archery tournament.

Verona was talked into signing up for the tournament.

The party knew that she was the best archerest by a long shot. The purse for first prize was forty gold pieces

There were only five people that entered the contest, other then Verona

They all shot their arrows but all around the bullseye.

When Verona shot, she hit the bullseye right smack in the center.

VERONA WINS!.

All the party gathered in the center of town and decided to stay for one more night.

That night for dinner they had beef and gravy, mashed potatoes, carrots, cornbread w/butter and jam, pumpkin pie, and excellent red wine.

The party was hoping they would not run into anything major on the way home.

Now that the party had plenty of rest, and had plenty of money, and their rations were restored, they started on their way home to Hollowfield to Castle Dragonshire to King Zandor.

That night they had just made camp, and a unicorn flew into their camp. The unicorn started talking to Glendora, because she could talk to and understand animals. The unicorn told Glendora that her babies were being taken one by one by some Ogres.

The ogres had heard that one of their own was killed by the hunting party, and they wanted revenge. They said that they would kill my young ones if the hunting party (you) would not come and fight. Glendora told the rest of the party, and they all agreed to help Mrs. Unicorn to get her babies back.

Mrs Unicorn said that if you do this for me.then she would fly back to the Castle and tell King Zandor that

Glanthria was ok, and will be coming home soon. You see the Unicorn could not fly Glanthria home, it would be using magic, and that was one thing she could not do. Mrs unicorn said that they had to travel through the swamps of regret, about three days away, over the ridge of rough terrain, and through the valley of dark Pinnacle Mountains. The party decided to walk at night, and rest during the day.

Glanthria flew on the back of Mrs unicorn at night, so if anything unexpected came up, she would be safe.

About sunset, the party reached the Ridge of Rough terrain. It was close to morning so they hid behind some rocks to rest. The next night, the party started out on their quest again. they reached the dark pinnacle mountains the next morning.

Again they rested.

The next night they pressed on into the valley, and saw the Ogres who were waiting for them. The Ogers rushed at the party swinging their clubs madly at the party.

Kendelyn snuck behind one of the Ogres and swung his sword, cutting off one of the Ogre's legs.

The Ogre fell to the ground and Grim ran up and slit the Ogre's throat.

Frateema ran onto one of the high rock peeks and jumped onto another Ogre, covered it's eyes and pushed it over a group of sharp rocks and killed it.

The third ogre tripped over its own feet and fell to the ground. Verona ran up and just stabbed it in the heart and it died.

The Unicorn flew down and Galanteria grabbed each baby, as they flew to safety.

After the young ones were safe, the party started their three day journey back to the forest,

The Unicorn took Galanthria back to the forest, to wait for the party.

Because the party was going to bring Galanthria back home as promised. Mrs Unicorn did fly to the Castle as promised..

Finally, after three days the party had reached the forest. They decided to rest for the night.

The rest of the trip was uneventful.

The party soon made it back to the Castle, bringing Galanthria home. King Zandor had his Guards arrest Queen Zorlonna, and the Queen demanded to know why. King Zandor said on the grounds of TREASON, and KIDNAPPING, ATEMPTED MURDER!.

King Zandor told the queen that he knew of the kidnapping plan and then of the plan to kill him.

Of course the Queen denied this, but one of her royal Guards had betrayed her to Father Authos, who told Cardinal Rusher.

Then The Guard threw the Queen in a jail.

As soon as the trial was over, King Zandor went to the village and asked Callie to marry him, after he had made Callie a princess.

As for Queen Zorlonna, she was stripped of her Royalty status, and was divorced from King Zandor Because of the charges against the Queen, this was allowed.

As soon as they could Callie and King Zandor were married, and Galanthria took her place on the throne.... FINALLY.

THE END

About the Author

My name is Charlotte M Schoff, and I live in Laporte Indiana.

I am the Author of "The WYNDS OF PASSION THE LOVE INSIDE" published by Phoenix Publishing, "THE LITTLE BOOK OF CHILDREN'S TALES" published by Cristian Faith Publishing, and "THE ROYAL HUNT Published by AuthorHouse Publishing.

I got the idea for this book from DUNGEONS and DRAGONS. I realize the game d&d has gotten a "bad rap" for being a "Cult game", but the game is just a fun role playing game.

I am hoping this book peeks the Fantasy side of everyone, and takes you to that place inside you where your imagination can run free. That special place where you can get away from reality, and just relax and dream.

Printed in the United States
By Bookmasters